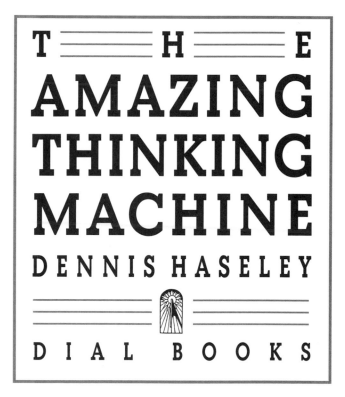

THE
AMAZING
THINKING
MACHINE

DENNIS HASELEY

DIAL BOOKS

Published by Dial Books
A division of Penguin Putnam Inc.
345 Hudson Street
New York, New York 10014

Copyright © 2002 by Dennis Haseley
All rights reserved
Designed by Lily Malcom
Text set in Berkeley Oldstyle
Printed in the U.S.A. on acid-free paper
1 3 5 7 9 10 8 6 4 2

Library of Congress Cataloging-in-Publication Data
Haseley, Dennis.
The amazing thinking machine/Dennis Haseley.
p. cm.
Summary: During the Great Depression, while their father
is away looking for work, eight-year-old Patrick and
thirteen-year-old Roy create a machine to help their
mother make ends meet, even as she is helping tramps.
ISBN 0-8037-2609-0
1. Depressions—1929—Juvenile fiction. [1. Depressions—
1929—Fiction. 2. Inventions—Fiction. 3. Brothers—Fiction.
4. Tramps—Fiction. 5. Poverty—Fiction.] I. Title.
PZ7.H2688 Am 2002
[Fic]—dc21   00-063860

*To my mother
and father*

CHAPTER ONE

Our father had gone to look for work, and at first I didn't understand. I thought work must be something you could lose like a marble and so just as easily find it where it had rolled, under a rock or in the bottom of your closet. Even after I turned eight and should have understood better, every night I still expected to look up from my bed and see him in our doorway, lit up by a smile, with a huge sack of bulging work, and saying what he always said: "Good night now, boys—and good dreams!" But Roy, who was five years older, said differently; Roy said Dad might have to travel far, and when he finally found work, he might not come back here but instead send for us to go there.

Roy said you could hear about such things over the crystal radio set that he and our dad had built. It wasn't like the big radio in the parlor. It was just a little metal board that had lit tubes showing; you went through the different stations by turning a neat thing that looked to me like the metallic jaws and teeth of a creature. Roy would let me do it sometimes; he would watch that I turned it very carefully and slowly until muted pops and a long eerie whine changed to the sound of faint and high-pitched voices, like mice talking. And then Roy would put the headphones to his ears and tell me the news he was hearing: that folks all over the country were out of work, lining up outside the factories; or that there were gangs in Europe who wore brown shirts and beat up on innocent folks; or that the Brooklyn Dodgers had defeated the Cincinnati Reds on a sacrifice fly in the ninth.

Usually our mother would poke her head in then, and we'd have to click it off. And as we were getting into our beds, Roy would say that even if we lost the big radio in the living room, even if it had to be carted away like they'd carted away Jimmy McCarren's sofa and table, they'd never get his crystal radio set.

Sometimes Roy got a little work himself—hawking papers or picking up people's old bottles and junk in his wagon. One Friday afternoon I went along with him to the junkman. We stopped by the vacant lot at the end of the next street, where our mom had told us not to go. And that's where I got my first good look at the bums.

They were gathered there, in what had once been a yard, among the weeds and the crumbling foundation of a house—young men and old, and some who must have been about our father's age. Several were standing; others were sitting around and talking, and when the wind came up, they hugged their knees. Some didn't look too bad, and were wearing clothes that might have been washed in the last week or so; but others were far beyond that, wearing tattered coats and overalls with rips that would let the cold air come through.

I looked down to my own self: plaid jacket, faded blue square over my right knee—the same way my father's jeans had been mended. "Don't they have wives?" I said to Roy.

He gave me one of his kingly looks. Roy had explained to me once that his name meant king in the country France, even though they pronounced it differently there. When he looked down his nose at me and there seemed to be something unpleasant that he tasted, I thought of it as his kingly look.

"What?" he said.

I shrugged. My own name was Patrick. My mom had told me it meant I was noble, but I wasn't sure I'd ever heard of a King Patrick.

"No, come on," Roy said. "What did you mean about wives?"

"To sew patches," I answered softly.

He laughed then, and everything was okay. When most people laugh, their eyes crinkle up. But when Roy laughed, his eyes opened wider—like he was seeing you clearly and he liked what he saw.

"They don't have families," he said. "They're bums."

I watched them, with their growths of beard, as Roy explained to me that these were not the same fellows as those lining up outside the factories. Those were working men. These were bums, and there was a world of difference between them. As he spoke, I saw one who was laughing, but not in an ordinary way—his laughter didn't stop, and kept going higher and higher. Another one was drinking something from a paper bag and passing it along. I thought I could see what Roy meant.

Then Roy walked away, pulling the wagon, heading for the junkyard by the tracks, and after a moment I ran to catch up.

Later, when we came back, it was starting to get dark, and we walked faster. When we passed the lot, we heard loud voices and the sound of breaking glass, and I could see fires in the trash cans, and the shadows of men with their arms extended, and ashes flying up toward the stars.

The next day, as we sat on our back steps swinging our legs, Roy said it was time to build something. Our father was smart, and clever with his hands; when I was still too little, he had shown Roy how to build amazing things—carved wooden models of airplanes and boats, a cart you could ride on and steer like an auto. Ever since our father had left, Roy had tried to build things on his own, in a part of the garage he had closed off with sheets and marked with a Keep Out sign suspended from a cord.

He didn't usually tell me about his projects or his plans. Now that he had suggested we build something together, I perhaps got too excited.

"How about another fort?" I blurted out. "How about a castle?"

He shook his head. He'd built the old fort with Jimmy McCarren and Robby Sinclair in a patch of trees not far from the vacant lot. It hadn't been up but a couple of days before someone carted it off. Roy figured the bums had taken it, to burn up the wood.

"I don't like to repeat myself," said Roy.

"Or some kind of machine?" I said. "Wait, how about a robot?"

He gave me a funny look—not the kingly look and not the laugh. I felt embarrassed. I still hadn't grown out of being a pudgy little kid, and the idea I'd suggested seemed small and unformed as well.

"Let's go see what Jimmy can come up with," Roy said.

We walked out to the front and headed for Jimmy's house. It was a bright Saturday in October, and there was a crispness in the air that made you think of apples.

Robby Sinclair's house was boarded up; he'd told us that he and his family were moving near to an uncle who had a farm out west and that they were really happy about it. Next door the Mullen sisters were jumping rope in their drive, and behind them their mother was throwing out some wash water from a large basin. Her grim face flashed a moment in its steel bottom; then she saw us and waved, and we waved back, and all the time her girls ignored us and sang a song of men without work:

> We don't care
> where we go.
> We'll pick spuds
> in I-da-ho.

Jimmy's house was four more down. As we climbed the wooden porch steps, Roy lifted his hand to press the bell but then he dropped it. He was a big kid for his age, with wide handsome features and almost-black hair. He turned toward me and winked and said it would be fun to pull a trick. I winked back.

Roy took a couple of steps to the end of the porch. The front bedroom windowsill of the house was off to the right, level with our heads and about three feet away. Roy stared at it a moment; then he leaned forward and grabbed its jutting wood. He held himself that way, keeping his feet on the porch, clutching the windowsill, out of sight of the door in front of me.

"Tell him . . ." he said, twisting around. "When he comes to the door, tell him I've been drowned."

"Drowned?"

"In the creek! Act upset." He scrambled a bit, his one foot dancing in the air until he again found the porch with it. "Just when he looks scared, give me the high sign."

"Yeah!" I said. "But what's the high sign?" I looked behind me to make sure that no one was coming down the street and watching this conversation between me and my brother plastered against the front of Jimmy McCarren's house. When I looked back, Roy had flattened one of his hands against the wall. "Okay," I said. "Then what?"

"Then I know to swing around and look dead and

scare old Jimmy into the middle of next Tuesday." His foot danced again in the air.

I stepped up to the door and pushed the bell. Then I rang it again because this was supposed to be an emergency.

I felt happy inside, and my heart was pounding when the door started to open.

It was Mr. McCarren. He was wearing a sleeveless T-shirt, and he looked like I'd just woken him up.

"Yeah?"

I took a step back. "Oh, hi, Mr. McCarren." I knew the trick was already wrecked: In an emergency, you didn't ask for a different person when the door was opened. But I figured Roy would want to take it as far as he could, so I kept on with it. "I'm sorry to bother you, but is Jimmy home?"

He half turned. "Jimmy!" Then he stayed that way; he didn't turn back like he usually would have and smile and ask me how that smart-aleck brother of mine was, or how my left hook was coming. He just stood there, facing into the dark of the house.

"Jimmy!" His voice came out like a bark.

He looked at me and shook his head, and I could see he hadn't shaved yet that day.

I took another step back and waved to Roy to forget it; it wasn't the high sign he'd shown me. But as the door started to close, Roy pushed himself back onto the porch and came swinging around with his eyes shut and his face all white and his head tilted to the side at a crazy angle.

He stood there a moment with his eyes still closed, making a gurgling sound. Trying to look like a drowned man.

"You little jerks," said Mr. McCarren in a dry and bitter voice, and then he slammed the door on us.

I ran off the porch, but Roy stood there a minute. Maybe he was trying to show he wasn't as scared or confused as I felt. We must have really bothered Mr. McCarren, and we hadn't meant to.

When Roy finally joined me on the street, he punched me hard in the shoulder, and tears came to my eyes. "Come on, Patrick!" he said. "Why'd you give me the high sign?"

"I didn't!"

"You did!" He showed me the wave I'd given him.

I didn't bother to mention how I'd seen his hand flat against the wall. And maybe I *had* almost touched the wall when I'd finished my wave. Roy shook his head. I didn't know if he was going to punch me again or not. I was bracing for it when we saw Jimmy McCarren walking down the street toward us.

We waited for him. When he was about two yards away, Roy said, "What's wrong with your old man?"

"Nothin'," said Jimmy. He usually had a smile pasted across his face, but it wasn't there today.

"Well, tell him we didn't mean no harm. We were just doing a stunt for you, and we got our signals crossed. I mean, Junior here did."

"Okay, I'll tell him," Jimmy said, starting past us. His mouth was a line.

"Hey, wait," said Roy. "The reason we came over— we want to build something."

"I can't," said Jimmy. He half turned away, staring up at his dark house, and I thought of his father then. "Maybe later. Not now." We watched him walk up his drive. When he had almost reached the front door, he looked back at us. Then he went into the house.

A minute later we heard him let out a yelp. His father wouldn't usually give him a strapping for something like that. Roy and I stood there a moment; neither of us seemed to know what to say.

Then Roy's eyes flicked away. "Look," he said.

Far down, from the next block, smoke was lifting up from the vacant lot. Roy cracked his knuckles, watching it. "Those stinkers," he said. "That's probably the front wall of our old fort they're burning now."

I waited a minute, till his words died away. As we started walking toward home, I said, "Probably the front wall," and spat once, in the bums' direction.

CHAPTER TWO

The next morning I heard someone shout my name, the sound seeming to come from inside Jimmy's house in a fading dream. When it repeated, I fully woke and realized it was coming from outside ours. My feet slapped on the cold floor, and I pushed aside the bedroom curtain and lifted the window. Roy was standing on the border between our yard and the yard of our neighbor Mr. Jonas. Scattered at Roy's feet were boards and lengths of beams, like a small forest he'd cleared and cut.

"You going to sleep all day?" asked Roy.

I dressed and made it outside as quickly as I could. Roy looked me up and down as I blew into my hands. He drew open the top part of my jacket and said, "Shirt's inside out."

"Mom's not up yet," I said.

He snorted. "I couldn't sleep much. I was thinking."

"About Jimmy?"

"About your idea. You said we could build a machine. I was thinking we could."

"That'd be great!" I shouted. All at once I felt happy again, and whatever I'd been dreaming or thinking was gone as if a page had turned. I stepped over some two-by-fours. "Where'd you get it all?" I asked, lifting a strip of wood with my shoe. The frost had melted beneath it.

Roy looked at the wood proudly. "Bobby Olsen and me got it from the lot." Bobby was a sickly kid from the other block. "While they were sleeping," Roy went on. "They only get what they deserve.

They'd stacked a bunch of it in the corner, right out there for anyone to take. One of them heard us on the last trip, so we just dropped the stuff and took off, but we got what we need."

"That's too great," I said.

Roy was lifting up a beam, carrying it farther into our yard. "What're you standing there for?"

"Beats me," I said, and I started dragging a long, wide board.

We worked all that morning. Mr. Jonas came out to help us around ten. He had retired from the railroad, but still wore his railroad cap. He brought some thinner nails than the ones we'd found on our father's worktable; these worked better in the wood. He showed Roy a way to drive them all the way in— "Drive them home," he said—to make certain the boards fit tight. When he leaned over and hammered or made a measurement, his breath started wheezing, like a squeeze box with a hole in it. Then he'd have to stand up.

On the ground we made squares out of boards to form frames; then we started hammering the larger sheets of wood onto them. When two of those were finished, Mr. Jonas sat down on a beam, resting as he looked off toward the sparse grass and few thin trees of our backyard. Then he got up and nailed the two walls we'd built so they stood by themselves at a right angle.

The back door of our house opened, and our mother came out on the steps. She wished a good afternoon to Mr. Jonas, and said it was nice of him to help with what we were doing. He doffed his cap and smiled and said it was no bother. Then she called us in for lunch. We were warm from our work, but Mom in her thin dress must have registered the early autumn cold. She put her arms around herself for a moment as she waited for us to gather the tools. As we traipsed up the steps, she ran her hand along our heads; I looked up and smiled, but I couldn't catch her eyes.

I hadn't realized how hungry I was until I sat at the wooden table our father had built. Mom had put mugs of Ovaltine before our plates, and I drank some down, too hot. She stood behind us, saying that if we didn't want to wait for her to go to the store for sandwich meat and bread, we could have the porridge she'd set aside for our breakfast, that we in our excitement had skipped. She was patting our chair backs as she spoke, in a way she had when she was bothered by something.

"Porridge for lunch?" I asked, at the same time as Roy said, "That's fine."

When I didn't say anything else, he kicked me in the leg.

"Okay with me," I said.

"So what are my boys building?" Mom asked as she brought out two white china bowls filled with the hot cereal, a pat of butter melting in mine.

"A machine," I said, as Roy said, "It's a secret."

She sat at the end of the table, watching as I lit into the food. Then she looked away, and her gaze went to the window and beyond, to the walls we'd put together, the pieces of lumber and the line of our father's tools.

"When you're finished—then you'll tell me?"

I shook my head no, as Roy said, "Sure we will."

Out back, after we'd eaten, I said, "You didn't have to kick me." Roy was standing in the corner where the two walls we'd made fit together.

"You don't have to be so dumb," he answered.

"Dumb? What am I dumb about?"

"You have to eat what Mom gives us." He shook his head. "Oh, you're just a little guy," he said. He poked my shirt button with his finger, then he closed up the top of my jacket.

About two o'clock Mr. Jonas returned with some scrap wood he'd found in his basement, and a candy bar for each of us. He also helped us set up a sawhorse, so we could do a more even job of cutting the remaining wood to fit the frames. He showed Roy how to saw through the boards propped on the horse, and me how to help by holding the end of the wood, being careful not to pinch it against the blade of the saw.

While we worked, he spoke about his railroad days—riding in the maintenance car, which everyone called the caboose. He told us about the shabby fellows who would sneak onto the freights, riding from one shantytown to the next; and about the train yard "bulls"—the railroad's private police—whose job was to chase them off. But then he said that two boys didn't need to hear about all that mess. What he really wanted us to picture were the long, sleek passenger trains, with their first-class cars, their club cars, and how once he'd ridden in one, with a gold stick in his drink and his steaming dinner served under a silver cover, and music playing and the people around him all dressed up. Some of the men even wore penguin suits.

By late afternoon we had two more of the frames built. One was covered entirely with planks; in the second we had left a small rectangular opening. We nailed these upright to the first two.

The thing we were building—this machine—had taken on the shape of a large box, with a gap in one side like an open door.

That night when it started to get dark, our mother made us stop working. I didn't want to tell Roy, but that was all right with me. I couldn't see so well, and the little nails Roy was letting me pound kept slipping away. And the hammer itself was getting too heavy; it was hard to hold it upright in my hand, as Roy was able to do.

When I came into the kitchen, Mom said she was going to serve us a quick supper of some cans of stew she'd stacked away. While I waited for Roy to come in from the garage, I sat at the table and drew circles in the dust on their lids. Mom tried to make a joke while she put out the plates. "Let's have stew for dinner," she said, and laughed, and when I said, "I thought that's what we *were* having," she answered, "No, *Stu,* like the name Stuart. Let's have *Stu* for dinner."

I took a second to laugh, and then we both did.

Roy came in and asked, "What's so funny?" and we both said, "Let's have *Stu* for dinner!" Roy watched Mom open the cans into the pan and he didn't laugh with us.

Even though she was trying to joke, I could tell that Mom was tired, by the lines around her eyes, the way her mouth would set when she wasn't smiling. I hoped that a letter from my father would come. It was when that happened that her face sometimes grew smooth again, like a girl's, and the liveliness in her smile seemed to come from inside. Or maybe when our machine was finally done—maybe that would do the trick.

CHAPTER THREE

While Roy helped our mother clear the table and wash up the dishes, I looked outside at what we had built. I still didn't know what it was supposed to do. From here it looked like not much more than a crate, with the dots of its nail heads gleaming silver from the streetlight. Roy said we were going to be putting on other things, tubes and lights, and I tried to picture how that would help. I couldn't quite see it, but another picture came to mind. It had to do with our father. I imagined him at that very minute standing by a lit-up machine with gears and lights and numbers and dials, and he was doing work with it—punching buttons and pulling switches and taking out amazing things like pressed pants and gleaming kettles.

Just when I started to smile to myself, I had a darker thought: that maybe it wasn't like that. Maybe whatever town he had gone to had rows of dead boxes like ours, and no matter how many levers he pulled, they would never light up or make sounds or turn out anything good.

"It's coming along," Roy said right beside me, and I jumped a little.

"Yeah," I answered. It was getting harder to make it out in the dusk.

"Come on," he said. Mom had gone from the kitchen, and I followed him out.

He led me to the garage. Our father's car was there, underneath a cover; for a second I thought Roy was going to lift up the cloth, climb in, pump the gas, and make it start. But he walked past the car and ducked behind the curtains he'd put up. He came out a second later, pulled down the Keep Out sign, and drew the curtains apart, nodding for me to enter.

There was my father's worktable marked with grooves and nicks from past projects hammered and sawed; scattered on its surface were odd bits of tubes and wire, metal and tin foil, and magnets and boards that Roy must have been saving for various gadgets and devices.

He pointed to a cleared-off area of the table, where there was a small metal box of tubes with coiling wires and a little lever with a black handle. "This is one of the things I built," he said. "It's a radio."

"Like the crystal set?"

Roy shook his head gravely. "Different than that," he said. "Here, I'll show you." He slid it near and started making short and long clicks with the lever. "Morse code," he whispered as he clicked away. "It makes letters and words, from the dots and dashes. You see, Save Our Souls—SOS. That's three short, three long, three short. That's what ships send out, before they go down." He clicked it out.

"How does it work?" I asked. "I don't see any plugs. Or batteries."

"You think every radio has to be plugged in? Or use batteries?"

"Well, sure, I—"

"Well, this one doesn't."

"How come?"

"Don't act smart," said Roy.

"Don't act smart, don't be dumb—what do you want from a guy?"

He shook his head. Then he half turned from me and leaned over the little lever. "Save Our Souls," he said, tapping out the *S* and the *O* and the *S* again as he spoke it. He faced me once more. "It's a . . . transmitter," he said. "It sends out. Didn't you hear the clicks?"

"Yes."

"I just sent out that message, and who knows where it could go. Anyone could have heard it."

"The president?" I asked.

"Sure," said Roy. "Sometimes I've sent out a signal, and the next night, I've heard an answer on the crystal radio. Like, I said, who's . . . who's got the highest batting average going? The next night, what do you think?"

"What?"

"Well, one of the baseball announcers said it, that's

what happened. He said, he said, 'Babe Ruth.' So who knows who hears it?"

"Dad?"

"Yeah, maybe. Maybe I could send him messages. I could tell him about the work we're doing, and if he was tuned in, he'd hear it all right."

"And if he had a . . . transmitter too, he could tell us about the work *he* was doing," I said right back. But the picture of Dad standing in front of a dark and broken machine came into my mind, perhaps in a place that was like a shantytown, and the next question just seemed to roll out of my mouth.

"Could the bums hear it?" I asked. I was sorry as soon as I said it.

Roy turned to me, and he wasn't laughing or looking kingly. His face was tight and pale. "Not them— that's a really stupid idea! Because listen—sometimes you *are* kind of smart, and sometimes you are *really* dumb." He drew a deep breath. "Dad could hear it. But bums couldn't hear it—they could never hear something like this."

"All right," I said. "I was just being dumb."

"That's better," Roy said, but he still looked bothered.

"What about the other one?" I asked, pointing.

He nodded, and went to the far end of the table. He picked up a wooden frame with a flashlight set inside; it was hooked with curling wires to a large battery. He fingered the flashlight's switch. "Remember that plane that crashed, on the West Side?"

"No."

"Well, it came down into a house."

"Wow," I said, and looked up, as if I could see past the peeling paint of the ceiling.

"Don't worry," he said. "This flashes them. Sometimes at night, when I hear a plane, I listen if it's getting too close. And if it is, I can run out here and flash them. To warn them away."

"Away from our house?"

Roy nodded.

I reached for the switch and he batted my hand away. I brought my hand up to my chest and started rubbing it. "Not in here!" Roy scolded. "A light like that—you can't see it, it goes so fast. It's safe to flash it outside; but inside the garage—I don't know how it works, but it could blind you."

"Oh," I said.

He opened the curtain. "Let's go."

"Can't we click the other one, though?" I asked. I pointed to the transmitter.

"Maybe. What do you want to say?"

I thought for a minute; once more I pictured my father, and this time he was smiling into our room. "Good dreams," I said.

Roy opened the garage door, and instead of heading for the warmth of our house, he walked toward our backyard, where the dark made the air seem even colder. We were too far away to see if there was any smoke coming up from the vacant lot. I knew it wouldn't make any sense to go there to look. If they didn't have a fire, they'd figure out some other way to keep warm, and maybe they didn't need to keep warm at all. Like Roy had said, maybe they only got what they deserved.

The box we had built was sitting there with the extra wood strewn around it. Roy walked up to it and ran his hand along the top edge. "This is going to be the best one," he said, but I still couldn't see why. It looked to me like a sad little house, with no roof and nobody home, something a plane could crash into. Or maybe a cold house for a bum. It seemed an awful thing to think, with Roy looking it up and down and grinning.

"What's it going to be?" I asked, but I ended with a stutter, as I was shivering in the cold.

He didn't seem to notice that, or my arms around myself, or maybe he didn't really care. When he turned to me, he had the satisfied look of a king.

"It won't be giving too much away to tell you it's gonna be something special. It's gonna be *smart*."

"Smart?" I didn't know what he meant. "You mean it'll do . . ." It took me a moment to think of the right word. "Will it do amazing things?"

"You bet it will."

We couldn't stay out any longer, as even Roy started showing signs of being cold. When we came in the back door, our mother called Roy into the living room. He stood quietly next to me in the kitchen for a moment; then he shook his head and went in. I walked to the doorway to watch, until he gave me a black look and I turned back into the kitchen.

I knew what they were doing: While Mom sat on the couch with a ball of yarn, she had Roy put his hands out so she could wrap the yarn around them, getting out the knots and curls. Roy had been more than happy to help our father on his projects, but to stand in the living room helping our mother, with the blues and pinks traveling up his arm, was something he hated. I sat in the dark at the table and spilled some salt from the shaker into my hand and licked it, while Roy complained and our mother answered.

"I don't see why a guy has to—"

"Because *I* have to," said Mom wearily. "As the older one, you've got to take up the burden. And you know that if I can finish this sweater and gloves—"

"Okay, okay," said Roy.

"Now do hold still."

After a moment he said in a quiet voice that I had to strain to hear, "Do you think it'll be very long?"

"I don't know," she said. "I don't think he can be away too much longer." There was a tone in her voice that was like the salt taste in my mouth.

I went out through the back door and around to the garage. Once inside I hesitated a moment; then I opened the curtains and walked through, over the Keep Out sign that Roy had let drop to the floor. He was inside with his hands tied up, and I was here alone. I picked up the transmitter; I touched the tubes, the black handle of the lever. Then I clicked it.

I could tell that the sound it made had no more power than a knife tapping on a stone. With one look outside the curtains, I held my eyes tightly shut and hit the switch on the light. When there seemed to be no extra gleam coming through my lids, I opened my eyes slowly. I moved the switch back and forth: There was nothing.

I put the gadgets back where I'd found them and walked out through the curtains, drawing them closed behind me. I wasn't so sure now, about being smart. Maybe I had liked it better not knowing so much, when I could believe what Roy had said, that we could transmit out, or make signals to planes. Or maybe I was just doing it wrong: Maybe that was it. If Roy was the one to do it, perhaps the machines would work after all.

═══ CHAPTER FOUR ═══

We sawed and nailed and set wood into place after school all that week, in what time we could manage before it started to get dark and our mother called us in for dinner. We finished two more wood frames, and these we tacked to the top and bottom of the structure. Other than the opening on the one side, the thing now had the look of a solid box, eight of

Roy's footsteps long, six wide, four high. Above the opening, Roy screwed two hinges: There was going to be a trapdoor here, for what purpose I wasn't sure.

Mr. Jonas helped us size and cut a rectangle of wood for the small door. Roy said it had to fit closely in the opening and not leave too much space between it and the box itself. After it was hung, Roy told Mr. Jonas that what he had done was great, but that on second thought he realized even the hinges shouldn't be so visible. Mr. Jonas wheezed and stood up from where he was kneeling. He seemed mad for a moment, and grunted, "Now he tells me." He took off his railroad cap and put it back on, then said it was okay, he had an idea. He removed the hinges and scraped the wood with his file. He screwed the hinges in deeper and nailed two thin strips of wood over them; now you couldn't see the hinges.

During the times Mr. Jonas was gone and it was only the two of us working, Roy told me about the bums. He said that bums had lots of different names and he tried to remember as many as he could that he'd read in the newspaper or heard in conversation or over the crystal radio set. So far he'd come up with hobo, bo, tramp, piker, prog, and vagrant. He still thought the best was plain old bum. "Why dress them up with a fancy name when they're hardly dressed themselves," he said, and I sniggered and added, "Without even patches."

As we sanded down the outside of the box—which we now called "the machine"—Roy would say, "A bum couldn't make the corners so square," and I'd pipe in with, "A bo couldn't figure out hinges." Roy would say, "A tramp couldn't hit a nail in straight," and I'd say, "Or even hold a hammer very long." Then we'd step back and admire our work, while the leaves fell around us. Roy gave me the job of brushing off any twigs or debris that happened to land on its surface.

By the end of that week, I understood what the hinged door was for. When Roy was satisfied with the way it moved, he opened it, gave me a wink, and scooted inside. What he had insisted on to Mr. Jonas proved to be important. While he was inside, with the door closed tightly behind him, you couldn't see the hinges or the spaces around the door unless you were Dick Tracy.

When he came out, Roy said that he hoped he

wouldn't always need to go inside, but that he would for the time being.

I stared at the cube of the machine and then looked back at him. "What do you mean?" I asked.

"You'll see," he said. "Just remember, I told you this was going to be amazing."

Roy scrounged other materials. Mr. Jonas had a battery that charged up the emergency signal he'd used on the railroad. He said if we were really careful, he'd let us put the battery inside our machine, but that it could give off a shock if we weren't on our guard. He also gave us a propeller from a model airplane. Roy brought out coils of wire from our father's worktable. He traded a wagonload of papers to the junkman for a box of radio tubes; some were black as dead stars, but Roy said they would do just fine. And although Roy wouldn't let Bobby Olsen yet see what we were building, he got a gallon of paint from him that he stored in our garage. One afternoon he brought it out and with two stiff brushes we painted the machine black.

"A prog wouldn't know how to paint," I said.

"Even if he did, he'd let the wood show through," Roy answered. And then he explained to me the importance of a second coat.

When we were finished, you couldn't see the door at all when it was closed.

After Roy was sure the paint was dry, he drilled holes in two rows along the top. He set the tubes in one, and a string of our Christmas lights in the other, that I'd last seen wrapped around our tree.

In the front of the machine, Roy cut out two slots, like the mail slots in office doors.

The next afternoon while I was brushing off the machine, Roy came out from the garage with the wires from his transmitter and the switch from his mounted flashlight. He laid them on the ground, along one of the black wood sides. "I was thinking we should have a switch to turn it on," he said. "We could nail on a covering for it and paint it."

When he saw me staring at the parts, he said, "You don't have to worry. I can always bring them back or get more material, and make that stuff work again."

I shrugged and didn't say anything.

"Well, come on then and help, and don't be a lug," he said. "Don't be a piker."

"I'm *not*," I muttered. I didn't move for a minute, while he lifted the lever and placed it on top.

"I'm just kiddin' you," he said, and reached out to ruffle my hair, the way our father used to.

We let Bobby Olsen look at the machine from our back steps, but we wouldn't let him get close to it. He stood there next to me—he was Roy's age but not much taller than me—and he sniveled and sniffed in the cold autumn air and squinted and said it just looked like a black box you'd put a dog in. Roy punched him in the shoulder, and dragged him closer until he could see the tubes and the wires and the model airplane propeller we'd hooked on top. Bobby was either impressed or too frightened of Roy to say anything else.

But I knew a little how he felt—that there were two ways to see what we were working on: Roy's way, and this other one.

After Bobby left, I went to the garage and brought out the can of black paint. It banged against my legs as I carried it, making little black drips on the leaves and grass. I found the places on the machine where we'd missed with the second coat, where you could see it was just wood and not sleek metal like we wanted. I went over those with the brush.

Something happened that night that made me wish I could understand things the way Roy did. Roy said he had some thinking to do, so we came inside early, before supper. Our mother's face was flushed when she saw us march in. She snapped up a folded sheet of paper from the table like she'd snatched it from the air. "I've heard from your dad!" she said, smiling.

"What'd he say?" we both cried.

Roy was quickly over by Mom, trying to get a look at the letter while she told him to wait. The paper was wrinkled and she smoothed it out between her hands; it looked like she had read it about fifty times. I sat on the floor and got ready to listen. But then I saw this other new thing in the room. Under the chair in front of me, against the bottom cupboard, was a basket, with a white cloth inside that had been tied and was now untied. It contained all sorts of cans of food and packets of crackers and cookies.

"It's dated two weeks ago," Mom began. "He writes that on his way back to these parts, he met a man." She was staring at the page, although it seemed she knew the words by heart. "And this man knows a man, who is friends and sometimes partners with a fellow, who might have a position open in his sales force for wire fencing." She held the letter tightly and nodded at it, smiling a little, like when she encouraged us to study hard for a test.

"But where'd we get all this?" I asked, nodding toward the pictures of roast beef and vegetables I could see on the labels of the cans, the likeness of a little English boy in shorts sitting on a stool and eating biscuits.

Abruptly, she looked over at me. Her smile faded. After a moment she smiled again and went back to the letter, but when she read again, her voice had changed. It no longer seemed a miraculous thing she was holding, but a simple scrap of paper instead.

"Your father says this is a kind of fencing that farmers need to learn about, as it's different from what they're used to. He has been assured that it will only be a matter of time, as it's very effective against critters and varmints."

"And against progs and vagrants," I said, proud for remembering the words.

"What?" she said sharply. "What did you say?"

Roy shot me a look, his face tight. Just as quickly he leaned toward Mom. "He didn't say nothin'," said Roy. "But what Dad said, well, that's great!"

"That's great," I chimed in, unsure what had happened. I tried to make things better again by pointing to the basket. "I know. This stuff—it's from Dad, isn't it? *He* sent it."

Mom looked to Roy and then to me.

"He would have," she said. The tiredness was back in her face.

Roy had trouble sleeping that night. He was pacing around, pacing around; sometimes he went to the desk where he did his homework and scribbled something. I finally sat up in bed and asked what was up, if he had heard a plane.

"I'm just working on the machine," he said. "I'm making plans for the machine."

"What are they?" I asked. "And how's it going to be . . ." I tried to remember what he'd said. "How's it going to be *smart*?"

"You'll see soon enough."

"A bum wouldn't see," I said sleepily, and lay back down. I felt good, still full from the cans of peas and hash that Roy had foolishly refused to eat. He may have started pacing again, but before I knew it, it was morning, and he was shaking me awake.

Downstairs, with the sleep still in my eyes, I watched him go in the hall closet and pull out our mother's old Royal portable typewriter, that had the letter *b* missing. Then he had me help him bring up a square of old carpeting from the cellar, which we'd been saving in case we ever got a dog. "And we're going to need your bell," he said, without even asking. Minutes later I was standing in the garage, shivering, and watching him unscrew the bell from the handlebars of my two-wheeler.

In school that day it was hard for me to concentrate on adding and subtracting, on the simple words in spelling. I kept thinking about Roy, who was in a class down the hall, doing much more difficult work: He'd once shown me his long division problems, hooked lines with numbers beneath them, running down the page. I wondered if he'd be reading about the strange things he'd been hearing over the crystal radio set—about Lucky Lindy crossing the ocean all alone, and what they called the brownshirts in Europe, who formed in gangs and broke people's windows. And I bet he wasn't concentrating so well either—that he too was thinking about the machine we were building. With everything he'd gotten to-gether, it couldn't be much longer until it was done.

When at last I walked out the big double doors of the school, it didn't seem the day had gotten much warmer since morning. The sky was the color of slate. Up ahead Roy was walking alone past the ball fields, heading home. When I caught up to him, I saw he had a large book under his arm.

"What's that?" I asked. I tilted my head to try to read it. "Al-al . . . Alcatraz!" I said.

"You shouldn't jump to the end of the word before you sound it out," Roy said. "If you don't want to be—" But he didn't say any more. We walked a little ways farther. *"Almanac,"* he finally said.

I didn't ask what it was, but he told me anyway: It was filled with names and facts and dates.

Rather than go right in the house and say hi to our mom, Roy and I walked around to the rear to check on the machine. We could see at once that something was wrong. Our mother was standing by the back steps; she had her arms around herself again, but neither that nor the way her eyes were glistening seemed just from the cold. Mr. Jonas was standing beside her, looking into the back part of our yard. He put his hand on her arm for a moment, as if to comfort her.

We started walking more quickly toward them, over the leaves. When they saw us, Mr. Jonas shook his head, but he let our mom speak.

"It's nothing to be worried about," she said.

"Is it Dad?" asked Roy.

She shook her head no. Then Roy shot a look at the black cube of the machine.

"Nothing about your dad," said Mr. Jonas. "Your mother just got a little shaken up, but no need to worry. Everything's all right."

"What happened?" I asked.

Mr. Jonas gazed down the block—as if he could see past Robby Sinclair's house, past Jimmy McCarren's. "Two of them came by," he said. "Looking for food. It's not a usual thing. They don't regularly come this way, but they walked right up to your door."

"Two bums?" said Roy loudly.

"Progs," I said, and my mother's eyes widened.

"No need to get upset," said Mr. Jonas, pushing back his cap and scratching his head. "Your mom wasn't expecting it, I guess, and when she opened the door and saw them . . ."

"I was just surprised," she said, and tried to laugh as if it was no big deal, no different than the evening she dripped tomato sauce on her white dress. But you didn't need to be Dick Tracy to see it wasn't like that.

Roy paced forward, his hands clenching. "What did they do?"

"They were talking to her. Going on and on. When they saw me, they ran," said Mr. Jonas. "By the time I got here, they were already half a block away."

"Talking to you!" Roy barked out.

"Yes, they were asking . . . for food," Mom said, and looked at Roy and me. "I told them that I couldn't help right now, that I . . ." She shook her head, eyes still glistening.

"Did they—?" Roy jerked his hand toward the machine, as if he hadn't heard her. "Did they mess with it?"

"Not that I saw," said Mr. Jonas, but Roy was already striding toward it, with me not far behind. He looked over the top carefully, checking that the tubes and lights were unharmed. He ran his hand along its sides, and back up around the top, checking the switch and cover he'd put on. He felt around the inside of the two slots he'd made, and then reached to the far left corner, where the propeller was set. He spun this once with his finger. With another glance backward, he reached for the bottom of the hinged door, opened it, and scooted inside. Mom and Mr. Jonas were far enough away that they couldn't hear, but I could make out what Roy was muttering under his breath as he crawled there, looking for any sign of them: "Bums, rotten bums."

"Rotten hoboes," I added.

He scrambled out and said, "Well, I guess it's okay," but his face was mottled with red.

Mom wasn't saying anything. She was looking from Roy to me to Mr. Jonas and back to Roy.

"They have some kind of code, these traveling men," Mr. Jonas said, taking off his cap. "A whole system of communicating. They scout out anyplace they think is likely—for food and such. They might observe when you least expect, from off that road, say." He pointed back to the houses behind ours and the road in front of them. "And if they see an opportunity, they'll be by. If someone's fed them, if a house has been friendly to their needs, then they leave marks—maps—for others of them. Bits of twig or rock—sometimes you or I could read it, sometimes not—and it tells them if a particular house is or isn't good for food or shelter."

"Shelter . . ." said Roy.

Mr. Jonas shrugged. With a last look to our mother, he said, "Well, I'll leave you all be," and walked back to his house.

Mom knelt down in front of me. "I don't want you to use those words," she said. "They are just men like any other."

"I won't say them," I promised, and she nodded.

But I noticed she didn't try to say anything to Roy. She only watched him where he stood, staring at our machine like his eyes could burn a hole there.

CHAPTER FIVE

The next day at school I could hardly stay in my seat, let alone concentrate on my lessons. I half ran home, again under a gray sky. Roy was already there—he must have left school early—and there were new lines running down from the tubes and lights. While I watched, he twisted wires onto a little motor behind the propeller, and fastened them to Mr. Jonas's battery inside, along with another motor he'd found somewhere that made a kind of chugging sound. This new one, Roy explained in his muffled voice from within the contraption, could go on and off.

"On and off?" I repeated, feeling confused.

"For when the machine is thinking," he said, leaving me in the dark.

He pulled the square of carpeting inside—"For a comfortable perch," he said—and back outside, he spun the propeller and screwed my bicycle bell to a point just inside the circle it described. He'd set the typewriter and a flashlight outside the trapdoor; now he knelt and pushed these inside too. Still crouching, he opened a paper bag, brought out some sheets of notepaper, and divided them into two stacks. One he laid inside the machine and the other he handed to me. He gave me a pencil and said to put it in my pocket. He tossed in the book I'd called "Alcatraz." He walked once around the machine.

"Anything I've forgot?" he asked, maybe more to himself than to me.

"No," I answered.

"It's time for a trial run," he said. He reached and pulled the switch. "This is the part only you get to see." Then he opened the trapdoor and disappeared inside.

I waited. The light was fading in the west, behind the back rows of houses, and the wind was rattling a couple of dead leaves in the trees, rustling the paper in my hand. There it was before me, this black box with gray tubes and lights on the top, and two slots like closed eyes. There was no sign of sound or motion coming from it, other than the slight turning of the propeller in the wind.

"Roy," I said. I thought if one of the bums came around now and dragged me off kicking and screaming, Roy wouldn't be able to hear or save me.

"Roy," I said again, a little louder.

Bit by bit, like someone waking up, the machine came to life before me. First the chug-chugging started from inside, and then the lights and tubes started to shine, and the propeller started whirling, dinging the bell that Roy had put just in range of the blade.

I laughed and shouted at how neat it was, as great as he promised it would be. But that hardly said it: It was the neatest thing in the world.

Then, over the noise of the bell and the propeller and the inside motor, I heard another sound.

It was clacking.

Out of the slot on the left a piece of paper appeared. It trembled there in the wind—waiting for me to take it. I walked up and pulled it out, and read the typewritten words.

OY,

DO YOU WANT TO ASK A QUESTION?

"Sure I do, Mr. Machine," I said, and laughed again at what Roy and I had done.

"Tell me . . ." I couldn't think of anything for a moment. "Tell me, Mr. Machine—tell me what day is today?"

I waited there, while the thing chug-chugged and the lights lit and the propeller spun, ringing the bell.

I took a step forward. "What *day* is *today*?" I shouted.

Nothing different happened, but I thought, even so, it was still good.

Another sheet of paper appeared in the slot. I reached forward and took it out.

OY,
YOU HAVE TO WRITE OUT THE QUESTION

I took the pencil from my pocket. I smoothed a sheet of paper over my knee and wrote, the lead point making little holes in the page.

What day is to-day??

I put it in the slot. It immediately came back out, so I figured it was supposed to go in the other slot, which must be the "in" box like you see on desks in offices in the comics. I put it in that slot. While I'd been writing my question, the clunk-clunking sound had stopped, but I hadn't realized until it began again after I put in my slip of paper. The machine started chugging again; the lights blinked on and off— which I didn't see how Roy could manage—and after a minute or so of the chugging and the typewriter clacking, my answer came out of the left slot.

IT'S EVERY DAY

I looked at the words, while the wind shook the page. At first I didn't get it; I felt like someone trying to read one of the hoboes' maps, and it was beyond me. And then it wasn't. I thought about how long it had been since our dad had left, and how we still got up without him being there and went to school, and came back in the cold with no word from him, and how the bums were still in the vacant lot at the end of the street, standing around or sitting and hugging their knees. And how the next day was just the same.

Now the answer seemed so strange and true that it made me forget about Roy being inside, for I never thought Roy could have come up with such an idea. Squinting at the typewritten answer with the hulk of the black box before me blinking and clunking, I felt I was in the presence of some kind of intelligent device that had really spoken to me—a thinking machine we had built almost out of nothing, that could see beyond what I knew and tell me things I could hardly bear to hear.

Then Roy pushed himself out of the side of the box, knelt on the ground a moment, and stood up, grinning.

"What do you think?" he said, and I wondered if he could see I was still a little spooked underneath the smile I gave him.

"It's too great," I said.

He laughed and shook my hand. Then he turned and looked at it. "Only we could have built it," he said.

At dinner I looked to the row of cans that had come from the basket—there were fewer now—and then to the stew we were eating. "On the church charity table there's all sorts of cans, and baskets—" I felt a sharp pain in my shin; Roy was looking down at the notebook by his plate as if nothing had happened.

"Yes?" said my mother evenly.

Walking home from school I'd seen them stacked up, just inside the church's open door; now in my mind I closed it.

I picked at the food, noticing that Roy wasn't eating. He was breaking a dinner rule, reading what seemed to be his math homework at the table. I didn't know why Mom let him.

"I have some news," said our mother. She was smiling now, but I couldn't tell if she was putting it on or if it came from inside. "Mr. Hemmert, at the dry-goods store, liked the samples I did, for the sweater and the gloves. He'll take more—as many as I can manage."

"Well, *that's* great," said Roy softly, and I felt the salty taste in my mouth again.

As if she didn't hear him, Mom went on to say that he thought pinks would be better for the ladies, with maybe some reds thrown in. I watched her and tried to smile back—as Roy wasn't. When I glanced over at him, I took a closer look at what he was doing. It wasn't homework. He was drawing the machine. Mom could probably see that if she wanted, but she seemed too caught up in the colors of wool, the number of pairs of gloves she was sure Mr. Hemmert would take . . .

Her voice trailed off, while Roy kept slowly making a line with his pencil.

"I'll leave you two to finish up," she said. "I'll see you in a moment, Roy?" She went into the other room. I heard her knitting basket open, then the clicking of needles.

After a moment I told Roy he didn't have to kick me so hard, even if he didn't like what I was saying.

He acted like he hadn't heard; he was still stretching that line.

"Why aren't you eating?"

"I don't like this stuff," he said.

"It's good stew," I said. "*Stu's* coming for dinner."

He shook his head.

"What are you doing?" I asked.

"Making some changes."

"But it works so great," I said.

"Good enough, for now," he answered. "But it needs some additions."

"Like what?"

"You can't even tell, can you, Patrick?" He lifted his head and looked down his nose. He'd told me once that in France, the kings put the word *le* in front of his name. "Le Roy," he'd said, and that was what he looked like now.

The next morning at breakfast Roy told our mother that we didn't have to go to school that day, that it was a special day for the teachers to be off, and hadn't she received the notice?

She said she hadn't.

It wasn't exactly like Roy to lie, especially not in a way that could so easily be caught out. And it wasn't like Mom not to wonder about it, not to look out and see if the other kids were walking up the block, not to ask if Roy was joking with her. She looked tired again, even though we'd just gotten up. When I told her she should finish her bread and jam, she said she really wasn't hungry—even though she'd seemed it just a minute before—and she pushed the plate toward me with a smile that clearly didn't fit the way her eyes were looking.

"I'm sure you want more," she said.

Roy watched her; then he looked away as I started to lift the bread to my mouth. I knew he wouldn't take any if I offered—he'd hardly touched the food from the basket, and the strawberry jam was from there. As the sweet taste of the jam burst on my tongue, Roy turned his cold eyes on me. It was then that the church door I'd closed in my mind opened wide, and I saw the cans there and understood where ours really were from.

"That's okay," I said to Mom. I pushed the plate back toward her.

When we got outside, I could see that a layer of frost had whitened the grass and leaves. I stood there blowing into my hands while Roy walked once around the machine, looking it over, checking to see if the cold had done anything to it.

He borrowed a drill from Mr. Jonas; he bored eight holes in the front of the machine off to the side, four each in two rows close to each other. It didn't take too much work with our father's thin saw to cut through them to make a fair-sized hole in the front of the machine.

"And that's for . . ." I began. I really wanted to know, but didn't want to ask outright and look so dumb as I had.

"Putting in fuel," said Roy, panting a little from the sawing.

He attached a hinged board to the outside to cover the hole. Inside the machine he nailed a piece of wood so you wouldn't be able to peer in through the fuel door when it was open.

He painted that door with silver paint he had found on a shelf in the cellar, and added some silver bits to other parts of the machine. In the morning light it looked like what it was: a wooden box sitting in melting frost. The eerie feeling I'd had about it the day before had all but disappeared.

Yet I didn't want to let that feeling go away. While Roy was inside the garage scrounging for more nails, I walked toward it.

"Mr. Machine," I said softly. I almost expected a piece of paper to come out, calling me "Oy" again.

"Mr. Machine, do you know where our dad is?"

I heard Roy's footsteps and backed away. "The switch cover isn't holding on so well. I'll have to buy nails at the corner," he said. He flipped a quarter with his thumb and caught it; it was perhaps the last of the money he'd earned. Then he started heading toward the street, and I followed.

There weren't any kids around—they were all in school—and it was neat to have the block to ourselves. Gray smoke was rising from the chimneys of the white houses all in a row, looking like a fleet of sturdy ships chugging ahead in formation.

But some of the ships were in trouble.

Roy didn't look over at Robby Sinclair's house when we walked past it, but I did. Several planks of wood that had been nailed in front of the windows had been torn down, maybe taken to be burned in the lot; the window glass was broken. And at Jimmy

McCarren's house the curtains were closed in the front windows; the side windows were dark. Their garage was padlocked.

I started to get a drumming feeling in my chest that increased as we approached the vacant lot at the corner. We walked past slowly and both of us stared. One was sitting on the ground, moaning and rocking back and forth. He had a wool cap pulled down low over his eyes, and I wondered if he had eyes there at all, or if they had been pecked out somehow like I'd once seen on a dead bird. A couple of others were standing by some wood that was on fire, and it scared me to think that it could have been the wood of our machine going up in flames, that they could have burned it as easily as that. I wondered if the ones who had spoken to our mother were there, and I wished I could do something bad to them, for the upset they had caused her. Then I saw one take a drink from a bottle and I remembered seeing that before, and I thought about how today was like every other day for *them* as well—which only made the drumming in my chest grow stronger.

All of a sudden Roy stopped, and I heard him pull in his breath.

"What?" I asked. "What do you see?"

"Shut up," he said. He leaned against the wooden fence that bordered the lot, looking at another group of them on the far side.

"Stupid progs," I said.

"Yeah, but shut up," he said again. He was squinting. "See that guy?"

"The one in the blue coat?"

"No, the one next to him. With the ripped boots."

"And all the whiskers."

"Yeah."

"What about him?"

"No, never mind. No, it's okay." He turned and shook his head. "I just thought it was Mr. McCarren."

"What?" I ran to the fence and stared. The cold was making my eyes tear; it was hard to see him clearly. "It's not," I said. How could anyone we knew turn into one of them? But the idea that it could happen—and that Roy thought it—made me feel dazed.

We started walking on.

"Dumb stiffs," he said after a little while. It was a

new word he'd learned, but when he said it, his voice sounded thin.

"It couldn't of been him," I said. We reached the corner, and turned into the warmth of the hard-goods store. "He never had whiskers."

CHAPTER SIX

Word had gotten out that we were building something. Roy said the only kid he'd told had been Bobby Olsen, but maybe others had heard us hammering and wanted to see if it was going to be another fort. That day after school, as Roy tightened up the switch cover, the Mullen sisters and several other kids came by our house. They stood out front, peering into the backyard where we were working. Soon another group—the Davis twins and their sister, Sally, and Bobby Olsen himself—tried to get a glimpse of our machine from our back-door neighbor's walk, their view half blocked by two thin trees.

"We'll show them a thing or two," Roy said, and laughed.

So that had been his plan all along: to show the others.

"They won't believe it," I said, and laughed too, so he would think that I saw things as he did.

While the kids strained to watch, Roy screwed a thick metal ring into the bottom of the machine in the back. He retrieved a long bicycle chain and lock from the garage and ran the chain from the ring along the ground to a tall, narrow tree. He circled the tree with the chain and locked it, pocketing the key. "We don't want those stiffs taking this for wood," he said.

"They wouldn't even know it's wood, since it's painted black," I said. He smiled.

Also from the garage he took the rest of the parts from what he'd called the radio transmitter and the flashing light; from his room he brought out his crystal radio set. All this he put inside the machine. I went up to the trapdoor and watched him. He was wiring them together.

Back in the garage he told me I was never to tell Mom that he'd been messing with Dad's car. Then with his jackknife he cut off a sizeable square from the underside of the piece of folded-over canvas that covered the old auto. He carried it out to the back-yard; we held it open between us and lifted the pale yellow cloth over the machine like a blanket.

Seeing this, the kids must have figured out that whatever the contraption was, there wouldn't be much excitement with it today. When I looked for them again, both groups had gone.

That night I stood a moment at our bedroom win-dow, making sure I saw the shape of the machine be-fore I crawled into bed. Then I pulled up the covers and said, "Roy." I realized I could see my breath when I spoke, which was something new for our room. "Roy?" I said again, watching it.

"Yeah?"

"It's cold." I wondered if I would be able to make smoke rings in our room before the winter was over.

"Pull up the covers."

"I did. How come you put those things in the machine?"

"Which?"

"The light and the radio, the things you built."

"I put them in because me being in the machine is just a preliminary stage."

"Oh," I said. "But what's *preliminary*?" The *p* sound made a puff, and I wondered if he had noticed it too, when he'd said it.

"It means it's a first part of things."

"First *part*," I repeated, to see the puff again.

"It means it's not going to always be me running it," he said.

"I'll run it," I answered.

"That's not what I mean," he said. "Think about the way I built those other things—the light to flash the planes, the transmitter. Now I've hooked them all together."

"Yeah?" I was trying to follow along, trying to believe everything he said, still not knowing where it was leading. When he answered, I felt chills start on my skin.

"I mean, you shouldn't be surprised if some time that machine starts thinking for itself."

The next morning I woke up early. While Roy was lightly snoring, I dressed quickly in the cold. Our mother wasn't up yet; with nothing doing in the kitchen, I went outside. I walked around the machine, brushing off leaves.

In the back of the yard, behind a line of brush, I found three stones in a row, and two twigs touching at an angle. I knelt on the ground. If you looked along the stones, it all made an arrow pointing to our house. I thought I knew what it was. Even though Mom had said she couldn't help them anymore, she'd done it often enough in the past that they had left this mark. I didn't know why she'd ever wanted to do that, except out of some mistaken notion; or why she'd said they were men like any other. That could be true of Jimmy McCarren's father; and true of our father as well. After a moment I stood and looked at our back window. When I saw that it was empty, I kicked and scuffed at the marker with my shoes. Now they wouldn't be coming back around. But somehow I still felt bad when I snapped the twigs beneath my feet, and kicked the rocks away.

Friday Roy let out word on the block and in school that there was something we had to show, and if anybody wanted to see it, they should come to our house the next day. By ten o'clock Saturday morning we had six curious kids standing in our driveway, looking toward our house.

"Let's make 'em wait," said Roy. We watched them through our front door for another ten minutes, until our mother said we either better let them back or send them home, that it wasn't fair to leave them standing in the cold. Although it wasn't too cold that day: The sun was shining hard, and there wasn't much wind, which suited our purposes. We didn't want the notepapers blowing away.

Roy and I finally came out and led them around back. The canvas cover was still on the box. It didn't look like much, maybe a trunk with a cloth over it— but maybe a magician's trunk too.

"So what do you have to show us?" asked Matt, one of the Davis twins.

"Just that," said Roy.

The twins took a couple of steps toward it, and Roy put out his hand. "Not so fast," he said, and they looked at him and stopped. Though they were as big as Roy, they were also a year younger, and neither as strong or fast. He'd proved it last year, fighting them both off at one time to get back a baseball he'd batted into their yard. He'd given Matt a bloody nose, and Mark had quit swinging at him and said, "Truce." Roy still mocked them sometimes, saying "Truce" when he saw them. They wouldn't want any more trouble with him, especially not in our yard and with Bobby Olsen there, who would be on Roy's side.

They went back into the loose line that had formed. Keith Manus, from the next street over, appeared from the side of our house and joined the others. "What's the show?" asked Keith. He was about Roy's height, and wore a blue baseball cap he was never seen without.

"You're right, it is a kind of show," said Roy. He looked at me and winked, and I was proud of him then, for being my brother and handling this crowd of kids like a barker at a circus.

"What happens when you go to a show?" Roy asked.

"You watch it," said Mark.

"Yep. But first, there's something else, right? You have to pay admission."

There was a groan from among the kids, and Matt Davis shook his head and started to turn away.

"A penny," said Roy. "Or something else."

"What else?" asked Sissy Mullen, while her younger sister clung to her sleeve and stared.

"Fuel," said Roy.

"What?" said Keith and Bobby Olsen together.

"Fuel," repeated Roy. He walked back and with a grand gesture he took off the canvas cover. It was the first time they'd had a good look at the machine. A couple of them said, "Wow," and someone whistled. It did look like something, with its slick black paint and tubes and lights and propeller, with its silver streaks like on a Buck Rogers spaceship and its switch and bell.

"It needs fuel for us to run it," said Roy. "We don't make any profit on this. You can put in a penny, or you can bring fuel directly."

"What kind of fuel?" asked Keith.

"Sandwiches," said Roy. "Cans of stew." I looked at him, surprised as the rest. "Hash. Chocolate bars."

"What kind of machine runs on food?" asked Sissy Mullen. I never liked her much, as she always thought she knew it all. But Roy was ready for her; what he said next quieted everyone.

"It's an Amazing Thinking Machine," he said.

They scattered then, but it didn't take them long to return. Some of them brought pennies. Sissy returned without her sister, who was a little frightened by the thing. She brought a nickel and a can of Boston baked beans that she said her father—who had a good job with a shipping company—had gotten from the actual city of Boston. Keith Manus carried a bologna sandwich in waxed paper. The Davis kids brought a penny and a Hershey's bar between the three of them. Two other kids I didn't know so well—one named Hutch and the other named Ronny, both small kids with patches on their jackets—came and wanted to see it for free. I said they couldn't. Of course Roy wasn't there to tell them now—he had climbed into the machine—but the other kids who had come up with the price joined in and told Hutch and Ronny that they had to put up or shut up. They grumbled and left, so it was fine.

I said I wanted to wait a little longer before we

started. My voice was shaking, talking to these bigger kids. It didn't help much to think that Roy was right there, because I was going back into the feeling that he was gone and I was alone with the black box. Bobby Olsen didn't come back, but Hutch and Ronny did, and they had a package of vanilla cream cookies and a can of Dinty Moore's beef stew.

"Where's Roy?" Sissy Mullen asked, and Keith nodded.

"He's out getting other customers," I said, which was what he'd told me to say.

The twins and their sister nodded; Roy had said most would understand how anybody would want to get more money or "fuel" if they could. After that, there was a little scrambling in the line, the Davis twins trying to get in front of Keith Manus, saying it didn't matter that he had come back first, because they had been there first in the morning. Sally Davis got them to calm down by sandwiching Keith between them.

Once this was settled, I knew no one would want to wait much longer, and the more I delayed, the more likely it was Roy would have to get out of there to warm up or go to the bathroom.

I walked up and threw the switch, and its wood covering came a little loose. I took a step back. This time it burst into life. The lights flicked on, the propeller started to turn, and the bell began to ding. The chugging came from inside, and whatever jostling or shuffling the kids were doing in line suddenly stopped.

After it ran for a minute or two, a piece of paper emerged from the left slot. I picked it out and brought it back to Mark Davis, the first in line.

OY,

DO YOU WANT TO ASK A QUESTION?

He looked at me. "What's it mean, 'Oy'? What am I supposed to do?"

"The *b* doesn't work," I muttered. "Just ask it a question."

"How many days till Christmas?" he yelled at it.

"Shoot, wait," I said. "You have to write it out and give it to me, and I'll put it in the machine." I handed him a pencil and sheet of paper; he wrote it in an awkward left-handed grip and gave it to me.

How many days till Krismas?

"Good," I said. I walked forward and put it in the right slot.

The paper disappeared. The machine chugged and chugged, and I heard a quick burst of chattering from inside, from the typewriter. A folded piece of paper appeared in the left slot.

I took it and walked over and stood in front of them. I tried to look serious, like a teacher. I opened the paper so all of them could read it at the same time.

"It says *fuel*," said Keith Manus.

"Shoot," I said again. "It needs fuel to think. Give it over," I said to Mark Davis, and he handed me the Hershey's bar. I went back and put it in the fuel door.

"Some hungry machine," said Matt Davis.

I ignored him and waited. We were all waiting: Sally watching with her wide baby-blue eyes, her brothers biting their lower lips with their upper teeth, Ronny staring with an intent expression on his small features. Finally a paper came out from the slot.

I was sweating under my jacket. I didn't think Roy had a calendar in there—just the book, the almanac. I was hoping he had counted right. If he was just one day off, Sissy Mullen would catch it.

Their attention had shifted to me. I opened up the message and read it aloud.

TODAY IS CHRISTMAS

"Naw, go on," said Mark. Hutch and Ronny started laughing. I felt heat coming up in my face, which meant it was turning red.

"We want our candy bar back," said Matt, but Keith pointed and said, "Look."

There was another piece of paper coming out of the left slot.

I walked up and pulled it out. Not wanting to be the one to read it—in case it was another foolish message—I opened it so we'd all see it at the same time.

FOR ME

A couple of them started laughing, but in the right way this time. Then the rest of them got it. And I could see the truth of what the note said, and that no one was really going to mind giving presents to a machine that could come up with things that cracked them up.

In the midst of my relief, I wondered how Roy had come up with such an answer; I didn't usually think of him as being funny like that. I looked back to the machine. The sun had gone behind a cloud and you could see the lights and tubes better now—they were going off and on in rows.

I allowed each of them to ask the machine at least one question, and even though I wanted to take a turn, I didn't. Keith Manus squinted his eyes and touched his baseball cap like a pitcher; then he asked it what was the capital of Pennsylvania. The machine wrote back, without any fooling around,

HARRIS URG

Mark Davis said he was going to ask it what was the capital of Europe. Sissy Mullen said not to, that Europe wasn't just one country. So he wrote out:

What are the capitals of Europe?

I put it in the machine along with his penny. There were long pauses between the clicks coming from inside; I knew Roy must be having trouble, and I wasn't sure how much his book could help him out. Finally the machine sent out a piece of paper that said,

A PENNY FOR EACH

Sissy said, "I'll pay for five," and handed me her nickel. I stood back and waited with the others, while Sissy counted on her fingers, chanting under her breath, "Paris, London, Berlin . . ."

Suddenly pieces of paper started shooting out of the left slot. We ran up and caught them as they drifted across our yard.

There were six sheets, one letter on each. Then I

saw why the machine had given her an extra one. If
you put them together they read:

E

U

R

O

P

E

Sissy gave me a sharp look, while the rest of them
laughed.

Hutch stepped forward. He wanted the machine
to name the state bird of Ohio, which the others
thought was too easy, the kind of thing they taught
everyone in school.

The machine answered right back,

CARDINAL

Bobby Olsen had returned. I saw him standing behind the others, looking hesitant to come forward. I asked him if he wanted to get in line now, but he said he still didn't have any fuel. I looked to the machine; it was quiet now, waiting for the next question.

"You can ask on credit," I said, which was the way I'd seen our mother pay at the grocery store.

He wrote, asking if the machine ever got any questions it couldn't answer.

The machine typed back:

NOT EVEN THIS ONE

and we all laughed at that.

We could hardly get enough of it. I think we all felt we really were talking to something amazing, and getting answers that were sometimes regular but often surprising. It was only the first day, and we were warming up quickly. Who knew the limit of what we could ask, and what it might tell us in return?

But when it was Sissy Mullen's turn, her face was set, as she tried hard to think of something that would stump the machine. She wanted revenge for EUROPE.

She licked the pencil and wrote out:

In what state is
Ulysses S. Grant,
eighteenth President
of the United States,
dead and buried?

I had a bad feeling when I put it in the machine, and felt angry at her for trying to ruin things.

After a little while, a piece of paper appeared, and I pulled it out.

FUEL, it said.

I'd forgotten to have Sissy put in her can of Boston baked beans. When I dropped it in the fuel door, it made a clunk on something inside.

Once more the bell rang and the propeller turned. After what seemed a long wait, a message appeared. I took my time unfolding it.

HE'S NOT URIED, it said.

I handed it to Sissy without saying anything. She smirked and wrote out:

In grant's Tomb in New York State, Dummy.

I shook my head as I read it. "You have to cross out the 'dummy' part," I said.

She did and handed it back to me. I put it in the slot on the right, although now it felt a little silly being so exact.

The other kids were watching me quietly. No one seemed pleased about what was happening.

I went back to get the next question from Ronny. But everyone started pointing at the machine. When I turned, I saw the tubes were lit up, and the thing was chugging away. I didn't know what to think. A sheet of paper appeared, and I stepped back and pulled it out.

MAY E HE'S NOT URIED IF YOUR THINKING OF HIM, it said.

Sissy tried to spoil that by saying the machine had misspelled "you're," but none of us paid any attention. She was smart, but it seemed—maybe to all of us—that the machine was smart in a different way.

Most of them wanted a chance to ask another question. But I was thinking about Roy cramped up inside, so I said we had to stop, that I had my chores to do, as did they. There was some grumbling among them—Sissy Mullen in particular wanted another crack at the thing, and Matt Davis said suspiciously that Roy sure was taking a long time to return with other customers. Then he yelled to the machine, "Right, Roy?" and his brother and Sissy laughed. But even if they figured he was inside, it didn't break the spell of it; they all wanted to know when they could come back.

I waited some minutes after they had gone; then I walked up to the machine and whispered into the slot, "Roy, it's okay. You can come out. They're all gone." The tubes were still flickering, but the motor inside was still, and Roy didn't appear. Again I felt like I was alone with the thing, just the two of us there in the light that slanted down through the trees, in the wind that was starting to come up.

"Roy," I said again. There was no response.

I wrote out on a piece of paper:

Mr. Machine. Tell Roy he can come out now there all gone

and I put it in the slot.

After a moment a note came out from the other opening.

FUEL

"Come on, Roy," I said, laughing.

I took a penny I always kept in my pocket and dropped it in the slot.

I waited. After another minute or two a cardinal landed behind the machine and started pecking at the earth.

"Come on, Roy," I said louder. I started feeling uneasy; I had the thought that if I opened the side door and looked in, I wouldn't see Roy, but just the gears and wires.

"Then I'm going in the house," I said, but I still didn't leave. I watched the machine for any kind of sign, and for a second I wished the other kids would come back.

After another minute or so, a piece of paper appeared in the left slot. I walked up quickly and took it out.

HAD YOU GOING DIDN'T I?

and then the side door swung open, and Roy came out laughing and saying he had to whiz so bad.

While he was gone, I scraped away the leaves from the nearby grass. Roy looked happy with himself when he returned. I asked him how he'd thought up all those answers, and his face got really serious. "What do you mean, *me* think them up?" he said, and he wouldn't get off it.

I watched him tighten the cover for the switch and reattach a loose wire to a tube; then we carefully covered the machine with the canvas. Roy had put the food and money aside, and we carried it all toward our house. Just as we reached the back steps, he put his hand on my arm.

"You didn't see any of them, did you, Patrick?" he asked.

"See who?"

"You didn't see any of them bums around, did you?"

I glanced back to where I'd wrecked the marker. "No," I said. "None of them were around."

He seemed content at that. Inside our house, he showed our mother what we'd gotten and explained how. She sat on a kitchen chair and watched while he put the "fuel" on the shelf, and when he turned around, she said, "If it's the price of admission, well, that's okay then."

At lunch I noticed Roy didn't hold back from eating what we'd gotten from the machine—the sandwich and the beans and stew—and that our mother didn't either.

That afternoon Roy brought out some additional equipment from the garage—gears and another chain from a bicycle, some heavier wire—and put them in the machine. He spent about an hour inside with some tools, hooking the stuff together in some way I couldn't figure out.

"How come you're doing that if no one will be able to see it in there?" I asked when he came out. He didn't answer.

When he was finished, we sat on the back steps in the cold and he said we had to make some other adjustments. That it wouldn't stay convincing, that the kids would get too suspicious if Roy was never around when the machine was working.

"Then someone else should be inside," I said.

"Yeah," he said. "We could try Bobby Olsen."

"Oh."

"Patrick, you're too young. You wouldn't know the answers."

"I could figure them out," I said.

"Sure you could, but not quick enough." He looked sideways over at me. "Besides, you're doing a good job taking care of it."

"Thanks."

"And don't forget what I told you. Bobby Olsen, that's just for now. That's still the preliminary part."

"It is?" I said.

He gave me a wink; then he went inside to wash up, and I could hear him talking to our mother, but couldn't make out the words. I stared at our contraption, thinking over what he said. It didn't look any different if someone was in it or not. One of the tubes was glinting in the sun, and right below it, on the ground, was a spot of red: That bird was still pecking around. I wondered what I would do if right then I saw the word CARDINAL come out, typed on a piece of paper.

CHAPTER SEVEN

One of the bums did come back around.

It was the next morning, and Mom was down-stairs, fixing us oatmeal. I had run out of socks, and with the same feeling as walking past Roy's Keep Out sign in the garage, I pushed through the door into the bedroom she used to share with my father. I was telling myself she might have some socks for me laid out on her dresser, balled up and waiting, and that my going in there didn't have to do with questions I had, and the rocks and sticks in the dirt, and the kicks in my shin.

There was my father's picture on the dresser, smiling from the shore of a lake, waving hello with a raised hand. My mother's jewelry box was open on a low table, showing rings and hair combs. The white window curtains were closed; the bed was covered with the same white material, one side of it pushed out strangely. I looked at my father's picture, smiling, waving. Then I stepped forward and lifted the bedspread. On the floor, shoved partway under the bed, was a brown suitcase with a bulging top that wouldn't close. I pulled it out and quickly lifted its torn leather cover. Inside was a pair of jeans and a gray shirt, one of the blue sweaters Mom had knitted, and white woolen socks. Underneath were three cans of stew and one of Boston baked beans.

I put on the same socks from the day before—they weren't so bad. And at breakfast I didn't ask about what I'd seen; I knew I'd only get kicked in the shin again.

Roy went to Bobby Olsen's house that evening to

look through his set of encyclopedias. When I came around back to check on the machine, that's when I saw him. The prog. I couldn't be sure it was one of them at first, because the light was already fading. He was standing on our back steps. The marker was gone; how could he be there? But the strangest thing was that he was holding the brown suitcase.

"Hey, you!" I called, and he turned. He was wearing some slouchy hat and long tattered coat, and you could see why he'd want the jeans in the suitcase, because his knees were showing through the pants he wore.

He stared at me a moment, and then quickly away, and I felt a jolt of what must have been fear go electric down my back, making my eyes blur. He was already running before my sight got clear again, running back past our machine, toward the houses behind ours, stealing my father's case and more— stealing the whole shape and height of him who I hadn't seen for so long. As he disappeared into the next block, I looked to where he'd been, and then around our yard. The trees, their branches clicking in the wind. The machine. There was nobody else out; it was like he'd never been there.

"Mom!" I yelled. "Mom!" I ran up and banged on the back door. After a moment she answered it.

"What is it?"

"One of them came around," I said. "A bum. One of them. And he stole Dad's case—"

"Stole Dad's case?" Her eyes were grave but she was trying to smile, and she kept glancing to the trees and back to me. It gave her whole face the appearance of being in motion. "Would you call it stealing if he needed it?"

"I don't know," I said. "I'd call it stealing if he took it without asking."

"And if he didn't?" Her gaze had settled on the rear of our yard. When she looked down at me again, her eyes were glistening, and her face had grown calm.

"Yeah, but he looked—"

"How did he look, Patrick?" she asked gently. She was ready to go on if I wanted to.

"Nothing," I said. I looked down at my shoes, brown and lighter brown in the scuff marks. I knew what Roy would do if he were here right now. He'd tell me to stop before I went any further.

When I looked up, her eyes met mine. "I'm coming on in," I said. "I want to open that package of cookies."

"All right," she said.

"Wait. I forgot. I'll be right back." I turned and went quickly down the steps and strode to the machine. I paced around it as Roy would have, checking it, trailing my fingers over its wood and tubes. It seemed the same. I looked back to our house—Mom had gone inside—and again to the box next to me. It wasn't different; I was. Feeling different. Thinking different. I so much wanted to ask it a question and just have it tell me I was being dumb.

From then on, Bobby Olsen and Roy took turns being inside the machine. On the weekends, sometimes one would take the morning and the other the afternoon; during the week, they'd switch off days after school. Bobby wasn't as good or as funny as Roy, but even if his answers weren't the best—even if he got the capital of California wrong and made a stupid joke about the national bird losing its hair—the fact that Roy was standing around outside the machine when it sent out its answers made everybody won-

der, just a little, if maybe the thing really was working on its own.

While everybody was excited about it, we sometimes got as many as ten kids lining up with their
bologna sandwiches and cans of hash and candy bars
and bags of potato chips. At night when we broke
open the stuff, we ate like kings.

Roy spent a lot of time trying to think up funny
answers to questions. He'd pace around the room at
night, saying, "Well, what if they ask me who's the
best hitter? Well then, I could . . . I could tell them a
football player; I could say the Galloping Ghost, because of the way he hits people over." He took a book
out from the library that told where famous people
were buried, and he walked around muttering,
"Abraham Lincoln, Springfield, Illinois; the poet Walt
Whitman, Camden, New Jersey; Thomas Jefferson in
the stately grounds of his beloved home, Monticello,
in Charlottesville, Virginia."

Neither he nor Bobby Olsen much liked school,
but now they would sit in our living room in the
evening and throw questions back and forth at each
other. Sometimes they'd try to answer seriously

where the first baseball game was played, or who Dolley Madison was, and other times they'd just dissolve in laughter. Our mother might stand in the doorway and help them out when they were stuck, and it was good to see her laugh with them once in a while. She had figured out another way to work with her knitting—winding it around the arms of a chair—and I was happy that she needn't trouble Roy now that he was doing this other kind of work.

But nothing that Roy or Bobby practiced helped very much, as the kids asked questions you could never foresee. And what I could tell from watching—standing out there in the cold and seeing the questions go in the right slot and the propeller spin and the bell ding and the tubes light up, and then the paper appear in the left—was that the best answers seemed to come up out of nowhere.

One hard, bright Monday, when everything seemed so stiff in the cold that it was like you clanged as you walked around, Jimmy McCarren showed up. He stood at the back of our neighbor's yard, looking down the block and then, when he thought we weren't watching, shooting glances at us. Bobby

Olsen had told us a rumor that Jimmy's father had lost his factory job, and that someone had seen him on a street corner, cadging a cigarette.

Keith Manus and Sally Davis waved at Jimmy, and he gave a hesitant smile, a shadow of the one he used to have. Matt Davis smirked and said something to his brother; then he took a step toward Jimmy and called out, "How's your old man?" Jimmy turned and walked away, and a part of me turned and walked with him.

Roy's mouth was set as he addressed the kids. "First question," he said.

It was going to be Bobby Olsen's first chance of the week. He hadn't been doing so well: Saturday he'd made a mistake about the positions of the planets, mixing up Mars and Venus, and Mark Davis had said the machine was losing its mind. And now Sissy Mullen was up. She had the question already written out on a little card like teachers use. She flipped it around for Roy and me to see.

If we say that someone with glasses has four eyes, then what kind of person has three eyes?

"There's no kind of person like that," Roy said.

"Nobody," I agreed.

"Yes there is," Sissy said.

"If it's not a real thing, you can't ask it," snapped Roy.

"Take a look at this." She reached in the pocket of her gray wool coat and brought out a picture of an Englishman with a lens in one of his eyes. "It's called a *monocle*," she said in a low voice.

Roy shook his head, and I looked down. I knew in all their questions back and forth, this had never come up. Bobby would never be able to type out SOMEONE WITH A MONOCLE.

"Why doesn't she get to ask the question?" Mark asked.

"You don't need to worry about it," said Roy. He turned to Sissy. "You can ask it," he told her, and she smirked.

She handed him the note, and he walked forward and placed it in the right slot. The machine chugged and the lights flashed off and on. And surprisingly quickly, an answer appeared in the left opening.

Before Roy or I could get it, Sissy ran up and

pulled it from the machine. "Not true," she cried, walking toward us, waving the paper.

EVERYONE, it said.

"Well, if that's what the machine says, that's what the answer must be," said Roy doubtfully.

"How?" asked Matt.

"I get to ask it how," Sissy said.

"More fuel, then," said Roy.

Sissy pulled in her thin cheeks, but she handed him another penny. Then she wrote out,

How can everyone have three eyes?

and gave it to him and he slid it through the slot. She waited there, tapping her foot. Again a paper appeared almost immediately, and she stepped up and grabbed it.

After she read it, she threw it on the ground and stalked off. The sheet blew away in the breeze. I ran after it, and knelt and took it from where it was flapping against a branch.

**THE TWO IN THEIR HEAD AND THE
ONE THAT THEY ARE**, it said.

I brought it back to the others in line, and let them pass it from one to the next.

"I never thought Bobby could think up a thing like that," I whispered to Roy, when I stood next to him again.

"Maybe he didn't," said Roy.

CHAPTER EIGHT

It rained for two days straight, so of course we couldn't do anything with our Amazing Thinking Machine. We went out a few times to check it under the canvas cover: It was staying dry. Roy was concerned that the water on the ground would get inside and float away the extra cans of "fuel" we were storing there, or stink up the carpeting, or rust the gears and magnets and springs; he cut deeply into the mud with a spade to make little rivers around the machine. And he brought in the almanac.

On the third day only a couple of kids showed up. I wasn't sure if the rain and the cold had cooled off their interest, or if their parents had told them to stop bringing us food that they themselves might be needing, or if the newness of the thing was just wearing off. Bobby Olsen's sister came by and said he had a bad cold—his mother thought from crouching inside the machine—so he couldn't help out again for a while. I wondered if he was really sick, or if he too had somehow grown tired of it. I felt the same as Roy, that the machine would never bore us. Of course, we had built it and were in on it, not just standing in front of it, stamping our feet, trying to think up questions.

But then our own interest did shift away from it. In fact, for a day we forgot all about the machine. Because our father finally came home.

He was sitting in the living room when we got back from school. At first I almost didn't recognize him; he had a light beard and mustache that closely circled his mouth, and he was wearing clothes I'd never seen him in before: a plaid shirt and clean, stiff overalls that looked like boards on his legs.

"Well, hello, boys," he said, and we both ran to him. Our mother was sitting down, then she stood up, looking from him to us.

"Your dad got a job," she announced, and she smiled suddenly in a way we hadn't seen for so long—an outward burst of happiness from deep in her heart. She started crying then, and my father put out his hand to her, and she sat back down and sniffled into a handkerchief. When she looked back up at us and smiled again, her eyes were wet and bright like she'd just come in from the rain. It was then that Roy stepped back and took a good look at our father, and perhaps seeing instead Mr. McCarren and other men we'd passed by, he said, "Why—why do you have that beard?"

"Keeps my face warm," Dad said, and winked, and hugged us to him again; but Roy, being older, pulled away.

By that evening our father had shaved and put on a pair of his regular pants with suspenders. He wiggled them up and down, and shook his head—there was space around his waist where they used to fit tight. He had brought home a fresh chicken; we ate it for dinner with mashed potatoes and canned peas that we'd gotten as fuel.

As we sat around the table, Dad told us about the job he'd landed. It wasn't the job he'd written us about; that one hadn't panned out. But he'd heard of a nearby factory that was hiring. "They wanted to get a good look at you first, though. They wanted to be sure about you . . ." He looked over at our mother, and then slowly over to me. "So I had to come up with some decent clothes."

I nodded and looked away; I didn't want to hear what he was trying to tell me. The awkward moment passed, and he went on, saying a man he had met on the trains had told him about the job. Now he was going to start in three days, on Monday. Yes, he said, he had met a lot of helpful fellows while traveling across the state . . .

"So what was it like?" asked Roy suddenly, his mouth still full. And then he kept going, like he was on a train himself, racing to someplace he had to go. "Riding in those cars, those first-class cars, like Mr. Jonas talks about. Oh, what do you call them?"

"Ask the machine," I said, wanting us all to laugh

and get back to our dinner. But Roy was going on like I hadn't spoken.

"The club cars," he said. His voice was louder than it should be. "So, how was it, eating food under those metal covers, with those gold sticks in the drinks and I don't know what all? And all the smart people you met there—how was it, talking to them? I bet some of them even wore penguin suits." He stopped then, and he was looking at our father, and he was blinking.

"Well," our father said, raising his eyebrows, glancing to our mother, then back to Roy. And his eyes softened when he spoke. "I did meet some awfully smart fellows riding on the trains."

Roy stared at him—their gazes held on each other for a moment. Then Roy threw down his napkin and walked out of the room.

Later, when I was upstairs, I could hear my mother and father talking from the living room: one voice and then another, the two of them blending, once in a while Mom laughing. I waited in the hall a moment. Then I walked into their bedroom. The brown suitcase was there, jammed under the bed. I eased it open; inside, along with the blue wool sweater, was the slouchy hat I'd seen on the man in our backyard. I walked into my room and lay down on the covers. Even though I'd worried it was so, now I felt stunned.

After a while I got up and went to the window. The light from the streetlamps made a dim glow in our backyard, and I could start to make out Roy. He was standing by the machine. I put my face closer to the glass. He wasn't just standing; he was leaning. His arms were crossed on it, and his head was down in them, and his body was shaking.

When I came down Saturday morning, the three of them were at the table for breakfast. My father was saying he planned to take a look at the workmanship on the device we had built. And as Roy nodded and I took my place between them, as my mother said she was quite sure he would be pleased with what he'd see, I wished that a photograph could be taken of us—that a man would put his head under a black cloth and capture our likeness in that moment when everything troublesome seemed to be forgotten.

After breakfast our parents went to the store. Roy and I walked out back to check the machine, to get it ready for our dad to take a look at it. The wind had blown the canvas cover half off, and when we got close, we could see there were little bits of twigs and seeds stuck on the black painted wood. The lights looked okay, but one of the tubes had broken. Roy pulled it off and took it into the garage to scrounge for a new one.

After a while he came back out and said he was going over to Mr. Jonas's. I kicked around in the leaves on the ground; now that Dad was back, he'd be raking them up. I knew that sometimes Roy took a long time when he was looking for parts at Mr. Jonas's. Maybe he'd be asking more about what it was like riding across the country in those sleek club cars.

I walked up to the black shape of the machine and looked it over. I was a little taller than it was. Other than the tube, it seemed fine. We could still bring our dad back when he returned. Maybe we could have him ask it a question.

Then I got an idea that made me feel better: Wouldn't it be something if I was the one inside the machine?

I looked around the backyards. No sign of any kids. No sign of Mr. Jonas or Roy. I thought Roy wouldn't mind if I went inside; I had looked in many times before, when I was with him. There was nothing he'd really care that much about, as long as I was careful—just the works he'd wired together, the tubes and the typewriter.

I walked alongside it, and felt for the cracks in the wood door. It was hard to see it; we really had fit the door tight.

After I located it, I reached down for the slot that Roy had put in, as a handhold. Just when I started to lift it, I heard a sound, and jumped back.

It was a sound from inside the machine.

I looked around our backyard. No kids, no Mr. Jonas, no Roy. No Bobby Olsen, sick at home. I shook my head and started back to the machine, but the sound repeated. I couldn't make it out until it turned to clicking—like a knife tapping on a stone.

I had the thought then that all the gadgets Roy had put in there were starting to work together—wires to tubes to batteries to magnets to typewriter to circuits to propeller to lights and back down to wires.

"Nah," I said out loud. But this time I didn't reach for the door; I circled around the thing once, walked all the way around its black square shape, over the little ditch Roy had cut, past the small piles of leaves I'd scraped off its surface. I thought maybe something had happened. Roy always said it could, like with the other things he'd tried to make: the airplane light and radio-wave transmitter. And the crystal radio really did pick up reports sometimes from the capitals of Europe—Paris and London and Berlin.

We'd worked so hard on our machine that maybe something *had* happened to it, inside. Other things had changed: Our father had gotten that job. And as I waited, I thought that all the rest of where Dad had been and what he'd done could just be forgotten, if only the machine would start.

A cardinal flew in from a neighbor's tree and landed not more than four feet from me.

I waited, as another minute ticked by.

I didn't want to reach for the door; I knew I should wait for Roy. But I finally gave in, and just as I began to lift it, the chugging started from inside and the lights came on across the top and the propeller started to turn, slowly at first, and then it picked up speed and began dinging the bell. The cardinal flew away, and I almost felt like running too.

But I stayed there, looking at the thing come alive, and for a moment I felt so happy again.

"Oh, Mr. Machine," I began. Then I said, "Shoot, fuel," and I ran off into the house; just inside the back door I grabbed a can of baked beans, and another of hash. I walked carefully toward the machine, one can in my jacket pocket, the other held out in front of me. I slowly opened the fuel door, dropped in the can, and then retreated several feet.

I waited there, watching, while the machine kept on as before, lit up and chugging.

I took a piece of paper and a pencil from my shirt pocket. I licked the pencil point, and thought for a minute. I didn't know how many questions I would have, so I wanted this to be a good one.

How will our father like his job?

I wrote.

Again, feeling a little afraid, I walked up to the thing and put the slip of paper in the slot on the right.

It didn't take long for the answer to come back, not typed, but printed out.

He will like it very much
Now go away

I shook my head, not understanding. Even if I was wrong, even if Bobby Olsen was inside, I didn't care—I didn't want this to end.

"Please, more questions," I said. I walked up and dropped in the can of hash, and the chugging and the bell kept on as before.

I was shivering now, from my excitement or the cold.

When will this winter be over?

I wrote.

I slipped it in the right slot. After not more than half a minute, the answer came out, written below my question on the same sheet I'd put in.

Spring the Vernal Equinox
will be March 21
Now that's all

I couldn't understand the words in the middle, but I could ask my mom later.

"One more, one more," I pleaded, knowing it couldn't even hear me. "One more and I'll go away."

I closed my eyes and thought hard. Then I quickly wrote out my last.

What will I be when I grow up?

The machine didn't answer for a long time. I stood there watching it, like the whole rest of the world had stopped and it was just me and this machine—this machine that I was believing in, and waiting for.

Then, for the last time, the machine did answer; the slip of paper did come out, from the same slot I'd put the question in.

Whatever you want, it said.

It made me so happy to read it. I felt the whole world start up again, even as the machine shut down—first its lights and then the propeller and the tubes. Finally the chugging inside stopped. Then I was just standing there, my hands clenched at my sides, looking at it before me, black and silent. The cardinal floated down between the branches and landed on the ground again. It was like nothing had really happened, like I'd dreamed it all.

I heard footsteps on the leaves behind me, and I turned and saw Roy. He had a couple of tubes in his hands, and a length of wire draped over his neck.

"What're you doin'?" he asked.

"Oh, Roy," I said, "it was working. It really was. I asked it questions, and it answered." I looked at the machine, then back at him. "Answers Bobby Olsen wouldn't have known. That you wouldn't either."

"Yeah, that's a good one," he said.

"No, it really did. I put in fuel, and it answered."

He shook his head and started toward it.

"Wait," I said. "Maybe we shouldn't open it up. Look." I ran toward him and reached in my pockets, bringing out the slips of paper.

"Spring the ver . . . the vernal—" He looked up suddenly. "Dad's in there," he said.

"No," I said.

"He would do something like that," Roy insisted. He dropped the tubes and wire on the ground. He walked up and pounded on the side of the machine; he smacked it roughly with his hands. "Come on, Dad, we got ya. Come on out now."

The machine didn't respond. Roy looked at me and smirked, and then he started to pull up the side door with both his hands. "It's stuck," he said.

"Maybe you shouldn't," I said.

He put his shoulder against the frame and gave the door a yank. It flew up, and he fell back with a yell. He lay on the ground for a minute, and I didn't move either, as we saw the guy come out of our machine. He crawled out slowly, giving me a good chance to look at him. He had a wool cap pulled down on his head, and his face was black with whiskers. There were patches on his coat, and our can of baked beans was sticking out of one pocket. He had tears in the legs of his jeans, and when he finally stood, I could see that one of his shoes was broken open, with a gray sock inside the flapping sole.

"Bum!" Roy cried out, scrambling backward. His face was twisted and red. He looked from the man to me. "A rotten bum!" he said.

The man was taking a minute to stand up straight, like there was pain in his back or his knees.

Roy was on his feet now, yelling at him, and from behind me I could hear Mr. Jonas's door open. "Get out of here, you dirty hobo!" Roy was yelling, and Mr. Jonas was calling out, "Get on away from there now."

The bum—the bo, the tramp, the prog, the piker—shook his head and wiped his hand over his face, trying to wipe away their words, or maybe the light of the day he'd come into. Roy was jumping around like he wanted to hit the guy, or give him a kick, when he turned.

"Come on," Roy said to me. "Come on! He was in our machine! Maybe he's wrecked it, ruined the insides!"

I started toward Roy, and then I stopped. I stood there, unable to move, as I had when the machine had lit up. In my pockets my hands curled around the crinkling messages this man had sent—the different words he'd used about spring. The kind things he'd said about my father, about me.

When Roy saw I wasn't moving, he gave me a terrible look—a look I'd never seen from him before.

"You think you're so blasted smart!" he yelled at me. "You didn't think it was Dad? Don't you know?

Well, I'll tell you something. That could be Dad—that could be!"

"I do know," I said. "One day—I saw him."

Roy stared at me, his face mottled red. "You're so dumb!" he said. Then he started after the man, yelling out what a tramp he was.

Still I stood there, looking at them, at Mr. Jonas trotting across his yard, at Roy running back toward the black box of our machine. Roy gave it a kick when he got near it; he swept his hand over it, shattering tubes, yanking out wires from the lights. Mr. Jonas tried to hold him back—Roy was cursing at the man, kicking at our black box, knocking in the door, cracking the fuel cover.

It hurt me so to see what he was doing that I had to look away. The man was hobbling from our yard. He looked worn and cold, no different than our father had looked. But as I watched him, I thought again about the things he'd written. They *were* truly amazing.

With a new row of lights flashing in my own mind, with all the tubes lighting up inside me, I saw in him what I'd never seen before, what Roy, blinded by his shame, still couldn't see. And I lifted my hand and waved—waved good-bye, but it wasn't just that. It was also hello. To him, and to my father. And most of all to what had been given to me—from that Amazing Thinking Machine.

═══ AUTHOR'S NOTE ═══

This book is set during the Great Depression, a time of sudden and severe financial hardship in the United States. Millions of people became unemployed—*thirteen* million by the end of 1932. Many jobless men—including heads of families—took to the road to find work, roaming from town to town by any means they could, such as hopping freight trains.

In 1929, when the Great Depression began, my father was thirteen, my mother eleven. My mother's father worked in the food industry and managed to keep his job, so they remained relatively well off. My mother recalls her mother feeding hungry men who came to their door; their house was "marked" as one that was helpful to those in need.

My father's family, however, was harder hit. His father was a machinist whose work was drastically cut back—to one day per week. He had to cash in an insurance policy to save the family house. My father started to work odd jobs when he was fourteen—distributing fliers, delivering groceries, and even releasing clay pigeons on a shooting range—in order to help support his parents and sisters.

Because money was so tight, my father's ability to continue his childhood pastimes required ingenuity. He and his friends used to wrap their worn-out baseballs with electrical tape so they could continue their ball games. And when my father wanted a bicycle, he scavenged in the junkyard near his house and built one for himself, out of cast-off parts.

My parents' childhood memories and impressions of this time, passed on to me, form the personal backdrop of this book.

Here are a few other notes to help explain certain references and terms for current readers: *Brownshirts* refers to university students in Germany, active in the 1920's and 1930's, who wore brown uniforms and were members of the National Socialist Movement, or Nazi party. *Lucky Lindy* was the nickname of pilot Charles Lindbergh, who made the first nonstop trans-Atlantic solo flight in 1927. *The Galloping Ghost* was the nickname of football player Red Grange, a three-time All-American halfback who became a defensive back later in his professional career. *Buck Rogers* was the name of a fictional rocket-ship captain featured in a comic strip and radio serial of that time.

The Great Depression is often described as ending either in 1933, with the new policies of President Franklin Roosevelt, or in 1941, with the United States' entrance into World War II. However, for those who lived through it—and for their children who heard their stories—it formed a lasting impression.

ABOUT THE AUTHOR

Dennis Haseley is the acclaimed author of more than fifteen books for children, including *Kite Flier, The Old Banjo, Shadows,* and most recently, *A Story for Bear.* He lives in Brooklyn, New York, with his wife and their son, Connor.